For Terry,
Some thought it was nowhere special,
but we went there and back again!
With you I shared the story of a lifetime.
R. C.

For Melinda,
who brought Eve to life for me.
K. B.

PUFFIN

UK | USA | Canada | Ireland | Australia
India | New Zealand | South Africa | China

 Penguin
Random House
Australia

Penguin Books is part of the Penguin Random House group
of companies whose addresses can be found at
global.penguinrandomhouse.com.

Published by Penguin Group (Australia), 2014
This edition published by Penguin Random House Australia, 2020

Printed in China

 A catalogue record for this
book is available from the
National Library of Australia

ISBN 978 1760 8 9773 4

penguin.com.au

With thanks to the Australian Council for the Arts for granting
the Australia Picture Book Illustrators' Initiative 2013 to the
development of this book.

Australian Government   Australia Council for the Arts

HELLO FROM NOWHERE

RAEWYN CAISLEY
& KAREN BLAIR

PUFFIN BOOKS

Eve thought that living in
the middle of nowhere
was better than living
anywhere else in the world.

She was never lonely.

Bluey waited patiently
under the saltbush for
her every morning.

Livestock rubbed against her leg when she called into the kitchen. He had to stay indoors so his ears and nose didn't get sunburned, which meant he was good to play with on a hot, hot day.

And Brian made her laugh when
she went out to the service station,
flapping his wings and fighting with
his reflection in the petrol pumps.

There were always plenty of people around.

The bus that brought everyone from everywhere came twice a day.

It brought Honey with her pretty hair and Johnno with his soccer ball.

It brought Gunther with his music, Richard with his swirling tattoos, and Sakura with her paper flowers.

Specials –
Chicken pie $9.50
Burger + Chips $12.50
Fish Basket

Caravans brought grandparents
setting off on new adventures,

and trucks brought truck drivers
with their stories and jokes.

Even when there was no one
around at all it didn't matter.

Eve liked to have
time just to run.

And to lie on a warm, flat rock
feeling the magic all around her.

Only one thing made Eve sad. She hadn't
seen Nan since they left the city long ago.

'Nan won't come out here,' Dad told her.
'She thinks it's the back of beyond.'

Eve wondered if there was
something she could do
to change Nan's mind.

Then one day she had an idea.

Eve tried not to get
her hopes up...

But with every day that
went by, her heart grew
heavier and heavier.

Then one day the bus pulled in...

'Nan!' called Eve.

Nan held her arms out wide,
and Eve gave her the biggest
hug she had ever given anyone.

At last Nan could see all the
things Eve longed to show her.

She met patient Bluey . . .

They found lovely, lazy Livestock . . .

And silly, funny Brian made
Nan laugh until she cried.

She met travellers from
around the world…

as well as the ones from up the road.

But best of all
she got to feel the magic.

One morning, Eve woke Nan up with the sun
and together they watched two hundred kangaroos sipping
dew in the long grass that grew next to the highway.

And one night they stayed up late,
and from down on the red-dirt airstrip,
they watched the universe go by.

Sharing everything with Nan made
Eve so happy that when it came time
for her to go she couldn't bear it.

Nan wrapped her arms around her
and held her close. Then very quietly,
she said, 'Don't worry, love...'

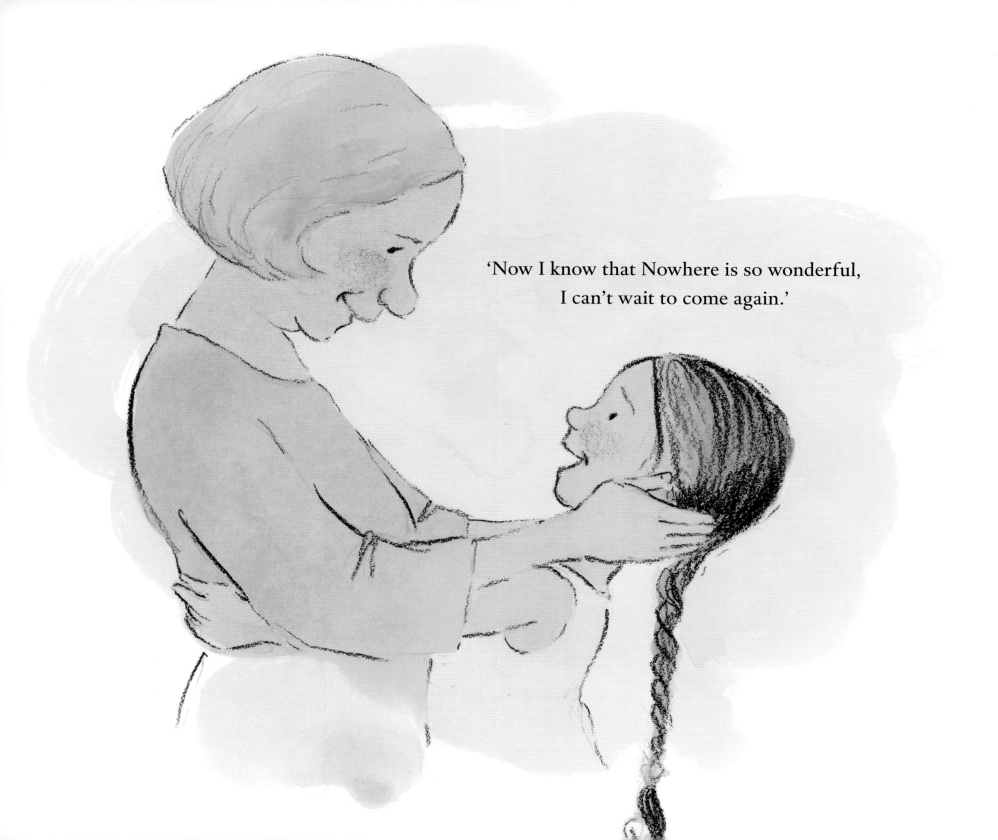

'Now I know that Nowhere is so wonderful,
I can't wait to come again.'